DOG ~~BIRD~~ RULES

Jef Czekaj

BALZER + BRAY
An Imprint of HarperCollins*Publishers*

For Annie and Ursie

Balzer + Bray is an imprint of HarperCollins Publishers.   Dog Rules.   Copyright © 2016 by Jef Czekaj.   All rights reserved   Manufactured in China.
No part of this book may be used or reproduced in any manner whatsoever without written permission except in the case of brief quotations embodied in critical
articles and reviews. For information address HarperCollins Children's Books, a division of HarperCollins Publishers, 195 Broadway, New York, NY 10007.
www.harpercollinschildrens.com

ISBN 978-0-06-228018-3 (trade bdg.)

The artist used line art drawn with ink on bristol and colored on an Apple MacBook Pro using Photoshop to create the artwork for this book.
16 17 18 19 20   SCP   10 9 8 7 6 5 4 3 2 1 ❖ First Edition

I think there must be some mistake, little one. I'm pretty sure that I'm a boy dog.
Ma
ma.
He's got your eyes.

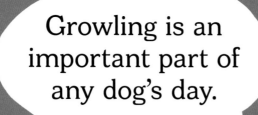

Being a parent can be confusing.
Tell me about it. I just ate worms!

Hmmm. . . .
Our puppy hatched
from an egg,
tweets, flies,
and eats worms.

Have we been
raising a baby bird
this entire time?

HA!
HA!

HO!
HO!

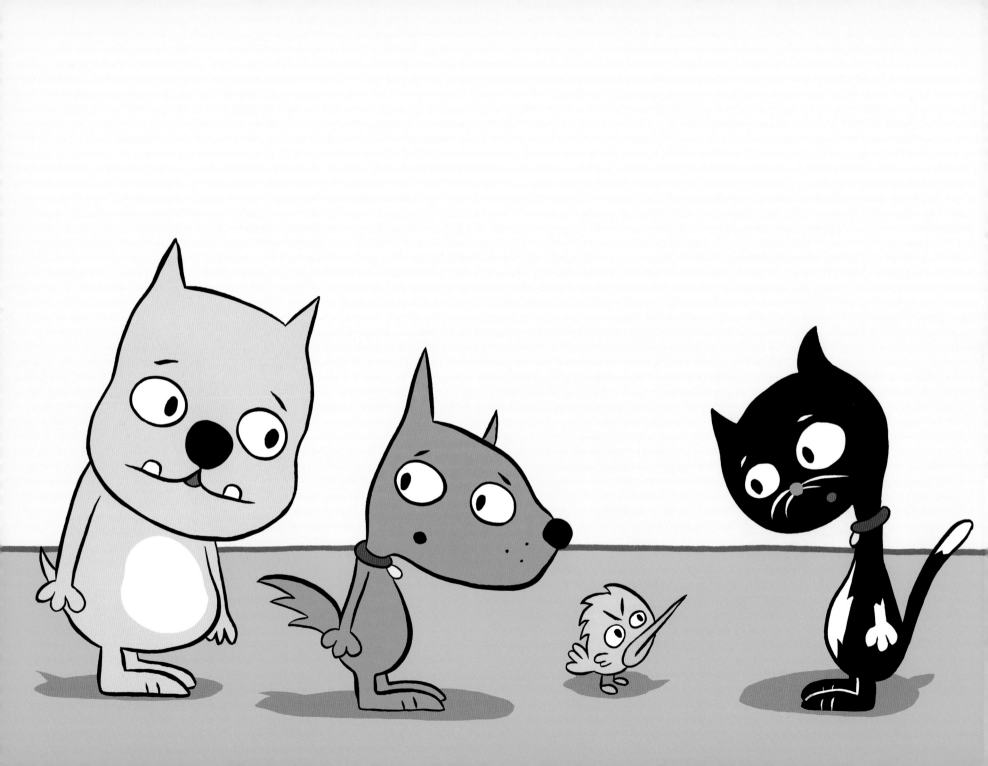